D0130934

Favourite Classics

Black Beauty

Retold by Sasha Morton
Illustrated by Jon Mitchell

Ticktock

An Hachette UK Company
www.hachette.co.uk

First published in Great Britain in 2014 by Ticktock,
an imprint of Octopus Publishing Group Ltd
Endeavour House
189 Shaftesbury Avenue
London
WC2H 8JY
www.octopusbooks.co.uk
www.ticktockbooks.co.uk

ISBN 978 1 84898 975 7

A CIP record for this book is available from the British Library.

Printed and bound in China

10 9 8 7 6 5 4 3 2

Series Editor: Lucy Cuthew Design: Advocate Art
Publisher: Tim Cook Managing Editor: Karen Rigden
Production Controller: Sarah Connelly

Contents

The Characters

Black Beauty

Duchess

Squire Gordon

John Manly

Ginger
Jerry
Little Joe Green

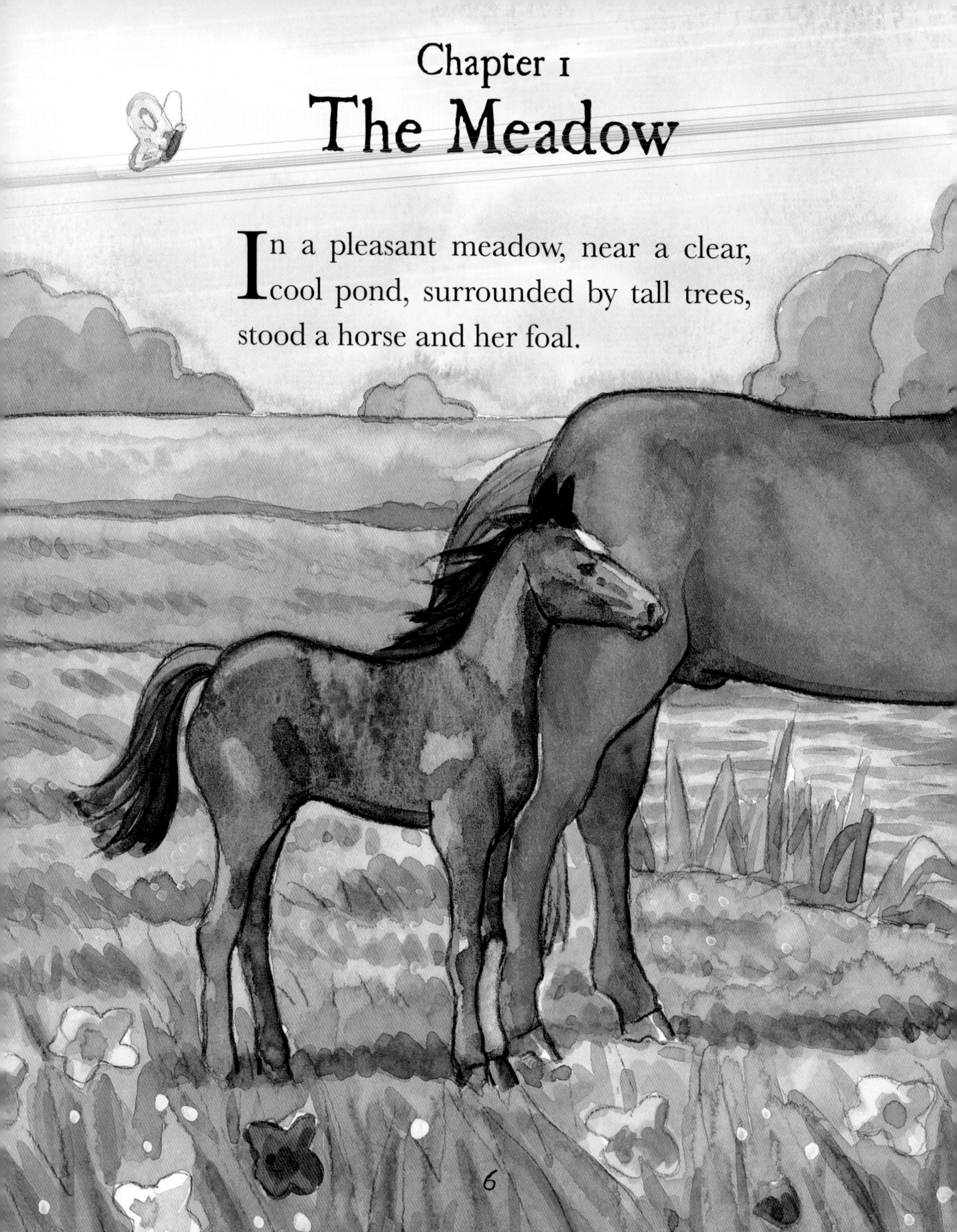

Chapter 1

The Meadow

In a pleasant meadow, near a clear, cool pond, surrounded by tall trees, stood a horse and her foal.

The horse was called Duchess, and she came from a long line of fine racehorses. Her foal was a handsome horse too. He had a shiny black coat, one white foot and a pretty white star on his forehead.

One day, when the foal was almost fully grown, Duchess's owner came to visit the meadow. He looked at Duchess's son, and was very pleased.

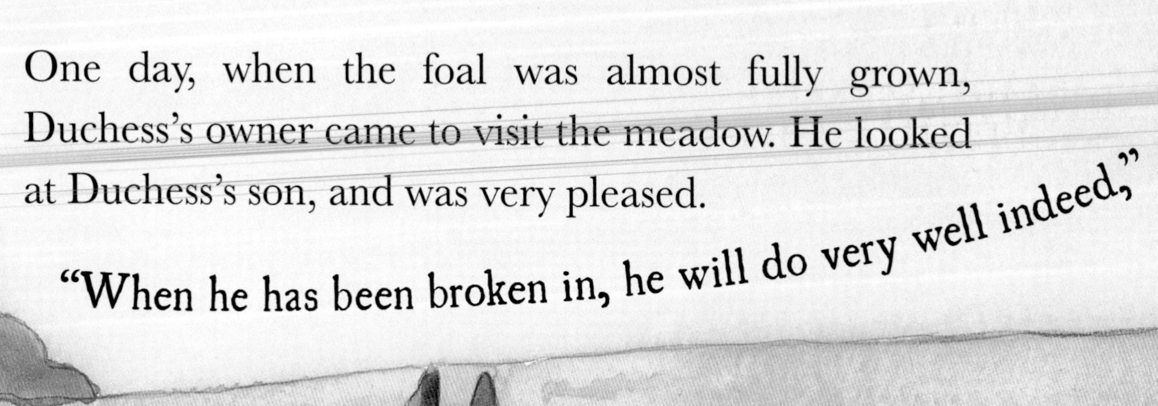

"When he has been broken in, he will do very well indeed,"

said Squire Gordon to his horseman. It was time for Duchess's son to be ridden.

The young horse was led around the meadow on the end of a long rein. Before long, he would be ready to carry his first rider.

Soon the handsome black horse had shoes fitted by the blacksmith.

Then he learned how to be ridden with a saddle and reins…

he learned not to be afraid of loud noises…

and he learned to pull
a carriage alongside
his mother.

Before long, Duchess's son was ready to take his place in Squire Gordon's stables.

He nuzzled his mother goodbye, then clip-clopped away with the master's groom to his new home.

Chapter 2
A New Home

Birtwick Park was a fine country estate, unlike the places many poor horses were sent. Everyone who worked there treated the Squire's horses with care and kindness.

At the stables, there was Merrylegs, a patient little grey horse who was the children's favourite, and there was Ginger, who was more elegant-looking, but had been badly treated in the past and was a little jumpy if someone annoyed her.

After just one ride, the handsome new horse became the favourite of both John Manly, the head groom, and his master.

"I have **never** ridden a better horse,"

Squire Gordon declared.

"We must give him a good name."

"What about Black Beauty?"

suggested Mrs Gordon. And that was that – Black Beauty was his name.

One grey Autumn day, John Manly decided to use Black Beauty to take the Squire into the town. The roads were wet, but Black Beauty made good progress through the deep puddles.

When they left town for home, the sky had grown dark and the wind was terrifyingly strong.

"I wish we were out of this wood," said Squire Gordon nervously. Just then…

Crack! A huge oak tree came down before them with a terrible crash. Beauty pulled up just in time, and the tree barely missed them.

The road home was now completely blocked!

"We'll have to turn back and go over the wooden bridge," said John Manly, guiding Black Beauty back to the crossroads.

But when they arrived at the wooden footbridge, Black Beauty pulled up and whinnied. The moment he put his hoof on the bridge, he could tell that there was something wrong.

John urged him forward.

"Go on, Beauty, what's the matter?"

he called, but Beauty refused to move.

The next moment, the gateman appeared on the other side of the bridge, waving a torch and shouting,

"Stop!

Stop where you are!

The middle of the bridge has been washed away!"

They finally arrived home after crossing another bridge.

"Beauty saved us from drowning!"

declared the proud Squire.

Black Beauty ate a hero's dinner of bran and oats and slept very well that night.

Chapter 3
Fire!

A few weeks later, Black Beauty went on his next long outing. Ginger and Beauty were taking Squire Gordon's family on an overnight trip.

Just as the sun was setting, the carriage turned into the market place of a bustling town. Beauty and Ginger delivered the family to their hotel, and then settled into a busy stable for the night.

But amidst the hustle
and bustle of horses
and riders coming and going,
nobody noticed a man
set down his lit pipe on a bale of hay...

A quiet, crackling noise woke Black Beauty. Something about the noise made him tremble all over. Beauty scrambled to his feet and saw the wooden beams above him were glowing hot and red.

The stable was on fire!

Stable-hands and grooms rushed in and led their horses to safety. As the flames rose, only Beauty and Ginger remained in the stable. Poor Ginger paced and whinnied with fear, and would not let the groom drag her outside.

Finally, bravely, Black Beauty let the groom cover his eyes with a scarf and lead him slowly into the yard.

Once there, Beauty let out a shrill whinny to let Ginger know he was safe. Not a moment too soon, Ginger came out. Seconds later, the stable's burning rafters collapsed behind them!

That whinny of Beauty's had saved Ginger's life. Yet again, the Squire's favourite horse had saved the day.

Chapter 4
Beauty Falls Ill

One night, Black Beauty was awoken by a panic-stricken John Manly. The mistress of the house had fallen desperately ill and the doctor was needed right away.

John quickly saddled Beauty and they rode hard through the gates of Birtwick Park.

There was no time to waste.

Black Beauty galloped like he never had before. The ground rushed beneath his hooves as they sped to the village. In no time, he was on his way back, this time carrying the doctor.

Black Beauty clattered up to the great house and the doctor headed inside.

At once, Beauty's legs began to shake and his coat steamed with sweat.

A young groom named Little Joe Green rubbed Beauty's legs and chest, but instead of putting a warm cloth on him, he left Beauty with a pail of water to cool him down.

Thinking he had done the right thing, Little Joe Green headed off to bed.

When John Manly arrived back at the stables later that night, he heard a terrible moaning. Rushing into Black Beauty's stable, he realised that the precious horse was terribly ill.

Beauty shook on his bed of hay, whinnying in pain from being left to get cold after the hard ride.

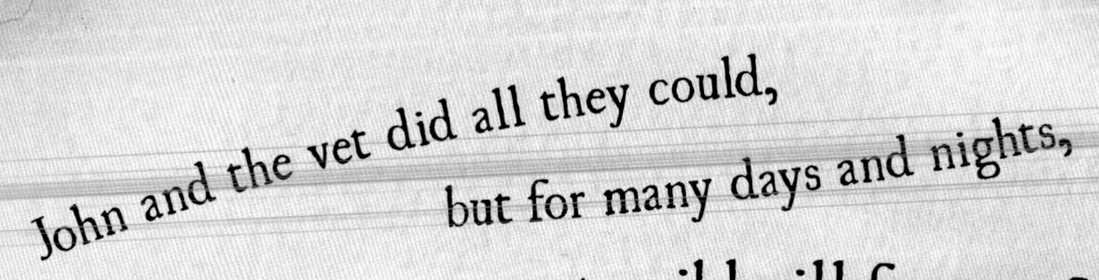

Black Beauty was terribly ill from a fever.

Little Joe Green was broken-hearted that he had put Beauty in danger, and John Manly was furious with him.

One evening, Squire Gordon crouched down in the hay and whispered into Beauty's ear,

"You did it, my lad. Your speed saved the mistress. She will live and so must you, Beauty."

As if he had understood his master's words, Beauty began to breathe more easily. And, when he realised Beauty would live, John Manly finally forgave Little Joe Green.

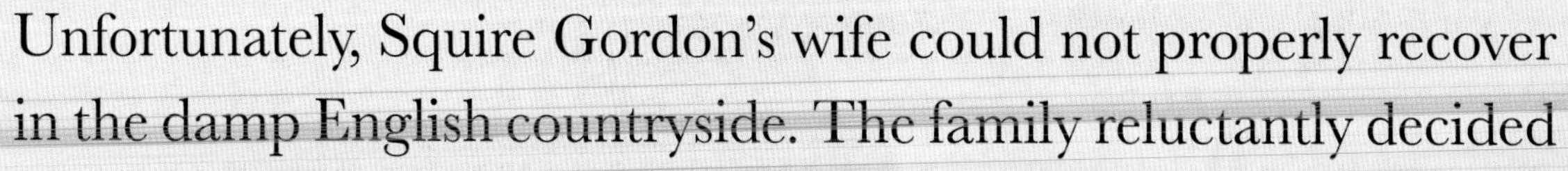

Unfortunately, Squire Gordon's wife could not properly recover in the damp English countryside. The family reluctantly decided to move somewhere warmer.

The house was to be closed up and the horses would have to be sold.

On their last night together, Ginger, Merrylegs and Black Beauty stood quietly in their stalls as John Manly said goodbye to them.

"Farewell, Beauty," John murmured in his ear.

Beauty whinnied sadly. He would never see his friend again.

Chapter 5
A London Cab-horse

A local family bought Beauty, but they did not treat their horses well. One day, a careless groom took Beauty out with a loose shoe.

Beauty limped along in agony for as long as he could, but eventually, on a stony road…

he stumbled...

fell...

and badly grazed his knees.

The mistress was horrified to find her new horse was injured – not because Beauty was in pain, but because he now looked less than perfect.

"I can't possibly keep a horse with scarred legs," she declared.

Beauty was taken to a local horse fair. Feeling worried about how poorly his next owner might treat him, Beauty waited to find out who would take him home…

Jerry Barker was a London cab-driver and a kind man. He didn't mind what his horse looked like, and he was the best owner a cab-horse could hope for.

Jerry rode Beauty into the city for the first time. Beauty trotted along nervously. There were tall buildings, glowing street lamps, horses and carts everywhere, and lots of people shouting and calling.

It was a world away from the peaceful countryside that Beauty was used to.

Finally, they reached a small side road, and an excited little girl ran up to them, asking,

"Is he gentle, Father?"

"As gentle as a kitten, Dolly!" replied Jerry. His children patted Beauty fondly. Beauty nuzzled up to them happily.

He was home again.

Beauty quickly settled into his new life as a London cab-horse. Jerry guided him carefully through the busy streets until Beauty knew exactly how he should behave. After just a few months, they made a great team.

They carried passengers night and day, from train stations to hospitals...

and from grand dinners back to beautiful homes.

Jerry's family treated Beauty like one of their own. Every day, Beauty saw how cruelly other horses were treated; they worked day and night with little food and slept in uncomfortable stables. Cruel cab-owners who beat their horses were far more common than decent ones like the Barkers.

Beauty was lucky and life was good,
until one wet New Year's Eve night...

Jerry and Beauty had spent the evening taking people home from one party after another. Finally, they waited at the last house for their passengers. Midnight came and went, the night grew colder. Beauty's legs began to ache from standing on the hard cobbled street. Jerry blew onto his frozen hands and stamped his feet. Finally the passengers appeared.

By the time they got home, Jerry was beginning to cough, and he soon became terribly ill with a chest infection. Jerry's days as a cab-driver were over.

Yet again, Black Beauty was to be sold.

Chapter 6

Beauty's Old Friend

This time, Beauty was bought by another cab-driver, but one who was as mean and impatient as Jerry had been fair and gentle. Over time, Beauty became shabby and thin like the other cab-horses.

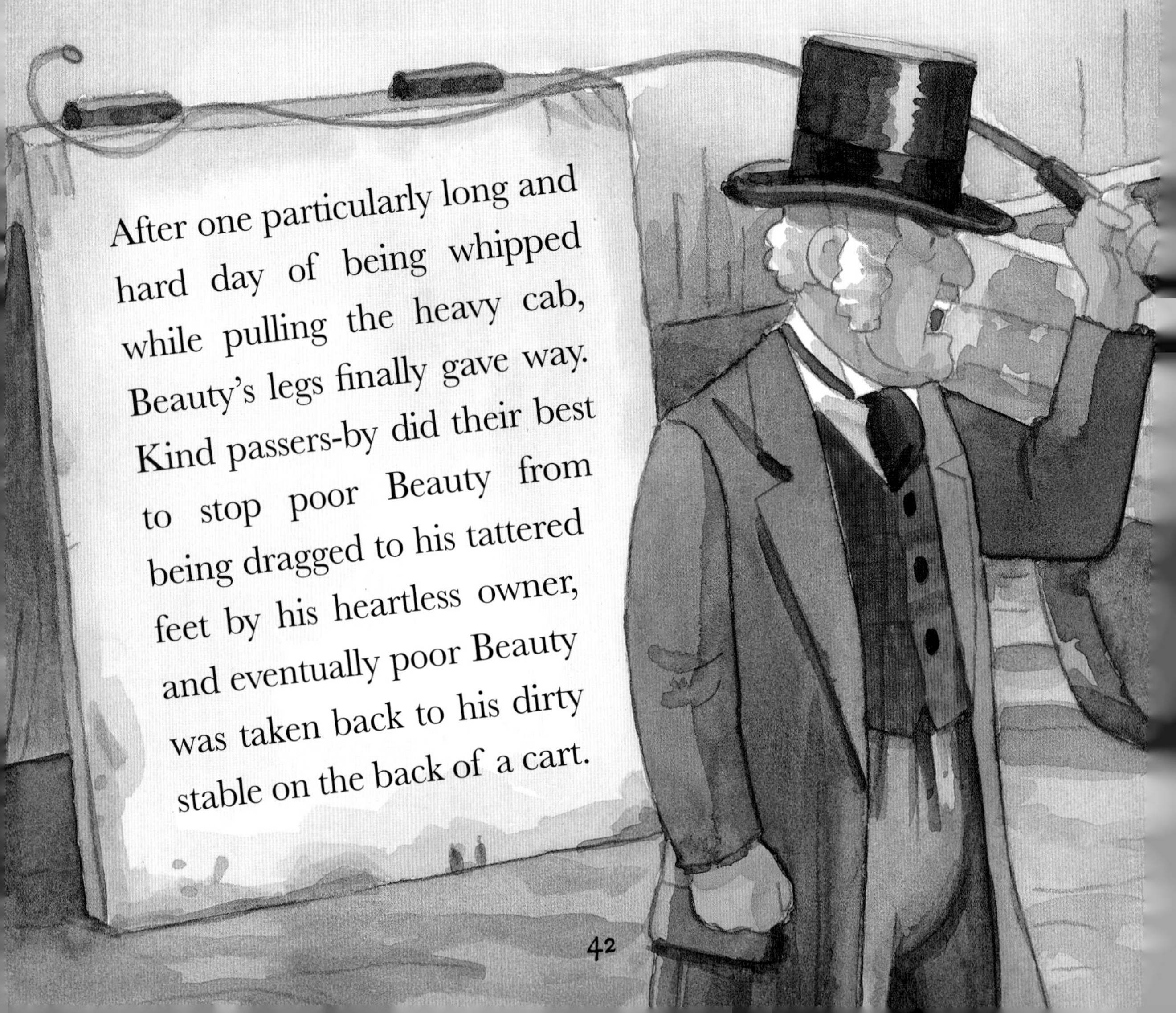

"I'm **not** losing money waiting for him to get better,"

complained Beauty's owner to the vet.

"He'll have to be sold."

So Beauty was
taken to a horse fair
outside London.

What would become of him now?

At the horse fair, a young lad took a liking to Black Beauty. He gave Beauty a friendly pat on the neck and Beauty nuzzled into his hand gratefully.

"Look, grandfather," said the boy, whose name was Will. "Couldn't we buy him and make him young and well again?"

"I should think he was a fine horse once,"
smiled his grandfather.
"Too many bad owners have
broken his body and his spirit.
We'll get him back on his feet again."

Together, Will and his grandfather began to restore Black Beauty to the handsome horse he had once been. After weeks of rest and gentle exercise in a soft, grassy meadow, Beauty was soon able to pull a carriage and be ridden again.

And on one sunny day, an old friend came to visit...

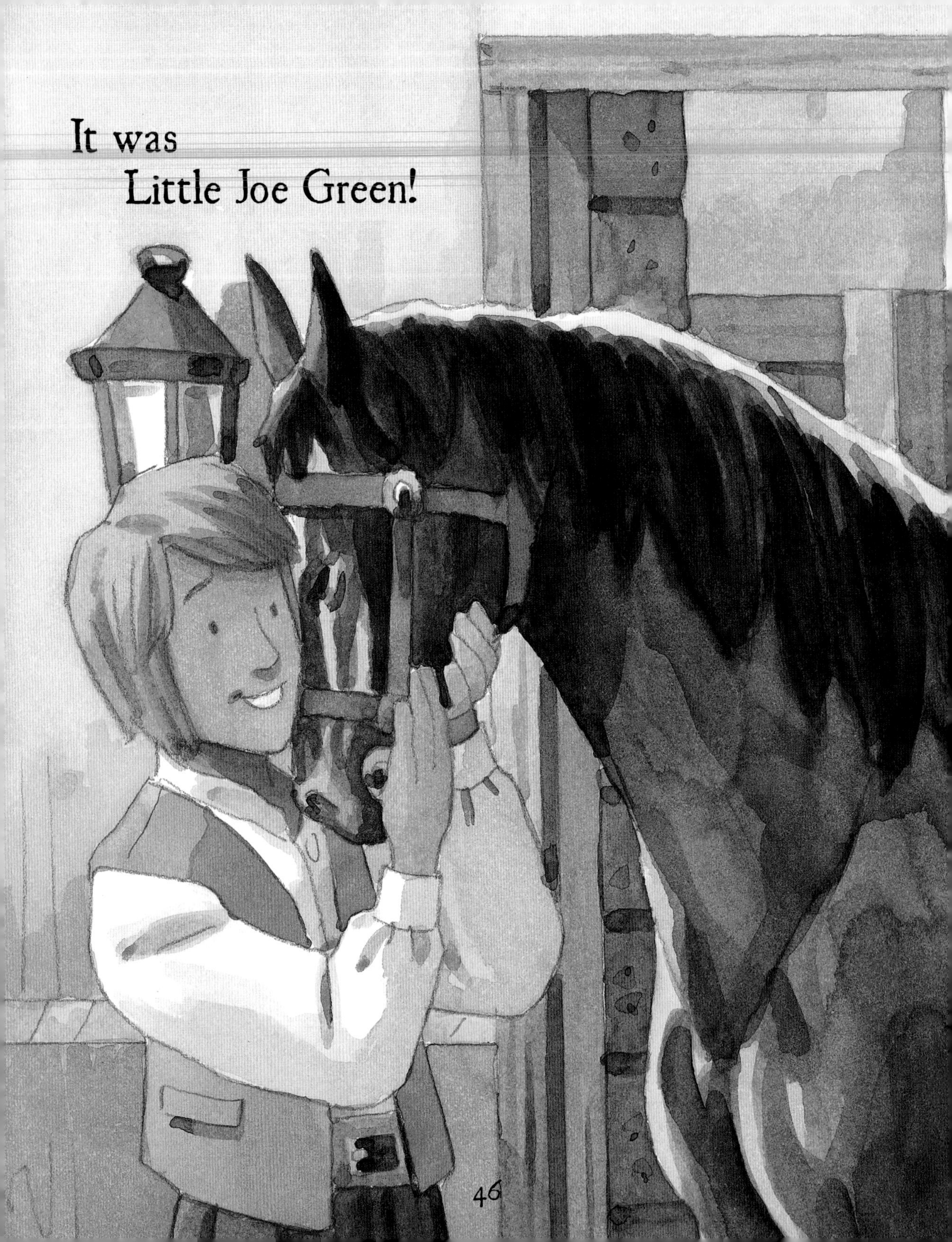

It was
Little Joe Green!

Now a groom for a local lady, he had come to see about buying an older, reliable carriage horse for his owner. Stroking Beauty's dark neck, he muttered,

"That is just like the white star
Black Beauty had.
I wonder where he is now...
Oh!"

With a huge grin, Joe threw his arms around Beauty's neck. "Beauty! It must be you!
It's me – Little Joe Green,
who almost killed you!
I wish John Manly was here to see
you too. I shall write to
Squire Gordon and tell him
I have got his favourite horse back at last!"

So it was decided, of course, that Beauty would return to the care of an older – and wiser! – Joe Green. At last, his world was a safe and happy place, filled with friends old and new who loved their gentle horse.

Black Beauty lived out
his days as he had begun,

in a pleasant meadow,
near a clear, cool pond,
surrounded by tall trees.